The Junior Novelization

Special thanks to Diane Reichenberger, Cindy Ledermann, Jocelyn Morgan, Tanya Mann, Julia Phelps, Sharon Woloszyk, Rita Lichtwardt, Carla Alford, Renee Reeser Zelnick, Rob Hudnut, David Wiebe, Shelley Dvi-Vardhana, Gabrielle Miles, Rainmaker Entertainment, Walter P. Martishius, and Sarah Lazar

The Junior Novelization

Adapted by Molly McGuire Woods

Based on the original screenplay by
Cydne Clark & Steve Granat

Illustrated by Ulkutay Design Group

Random House 🏠 New York

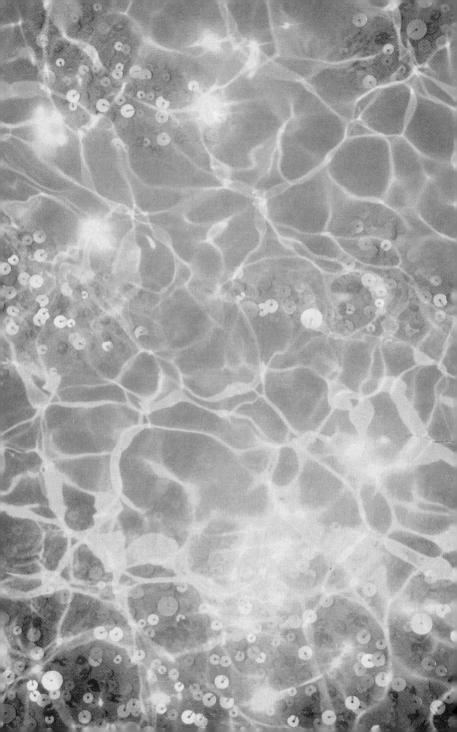

Chapter 1

Lumina the mermaid swam around her sea cave's front yard, collecting shells and placing them on a pretend throne. Her best friend, a pink sea horse named Kuda, fashioned a tiara out of a clamshell. They were playing their favorite game: Mermaid Princesses.

"What do you think, Kuda? Is it regal enough for a coronation?" Lumina asked, rolling out a red carpet made from sea flowers.

Kuda draped a purple sea fan around her neck like a cape. "Excellent. When I am crowned Princess of the Sea, I shall make you Chief of Royal Awesomeness," the sea horse announced.

Lumina chuckled, looking at the throne. It glistened with sea pearls, the same kind that dotted her long golden-blond hair. "I don't know," she said, cocking her head in thought. "It still needs something." Then she raised her fingers and wiggled them, as if casting a spell.

Suddenly, the pearls magically glowed! Next, Lumina reached into the pearl waist pouch she always wore. She retrieved a fistful of pearls and flung them through the water. Like a conductor, she commanded the pearls to drape across the throne like twinkly lights, each one gleaming brightly. It was beautiful.

"Now it's perfect! Shall we begin, Your Mini-Majesty?" Lumina asked, curtseying in Kuda's direction.

"Oh, let's do," Kuda replied, nodding regally. "Alert the royal subjects."

Lumina smiled as a group of hermit crabs, oysters, and fish crowded into the courtyard to witness the make-believe coronation. Every time they played this game, Lumina wished she were a real mermaid princess who wore fancy gowns and lived in a palace. Not that living with her aunt on the outskirts of town was a bad thing. It just wasn't very exciting.

Lumina longed to see things she'd never seen, explore places she'd never been, and meet people she'd never met. But her aunt Scylla wanted her to stay close to home, where it was safe. *Someday,* Lumina thought as she picked up the clamshell tiara. She watched Kuda make her grand entrance. A pair of swordfish raised their heads to let the sea horse pass, as though she were passing beneath real royal swords.

Lumina curtseyed again as Kuda arrived at the throne. "With the power vested in me by nobody in particular, I hereby crown you Princess Kuda, Ruler of the Seven Seas!" she said, setting the tiara carefully on the sea horse's head. Then she reached into her waist purse and tossed more pearls into the water. Lumina swirled them around Kuda's head and settled them atop her tiara. With a snap of her fingers—*ting!*—the pearls sparkled and glowed warmly.

"Thank you, thank you, my loyal subjects," Kuda said, quieting the crowd with her fins. "Ladies and jellyfish, let us celebrate my coronation with a royal ball."

Lumina offered her hand to Kuda. "Shall we dance, milady?" she said with a giggle. The ball was Lumina's favorite part of their game. She loved to imagine a real royal ball held in the nearby kingdom of Seagundia's palace. The gowns, the orchestra, the royal family: what a sight it must be! *One day,* Lumina thought, *I will see it for myself.* She only hoped it would be as beautiful as it was in her dreams.

"Lumina!" The familiar voice jolted Lumina back to the present. She shot Kuda a look and waved her arms frantically, directing all the pearls back to their oyster shells and into her purse. The crabs, fish, and other "guests" scampered away just as her aunt Scylla opened the cave's front door.

"Lumina! What was all that commotion?" Aunt Scylla said, looking around the water for the source of all the noise.

Lumina twisted her hands behind her back. "Um? Oh, we were just playing coronation, Aunt Scylla."

Her aunt nodded, unsurprised. "Ah. Well, I

need help with the kelp cake, so please come join me in the kitchen."

Lumina nodded and headed for the door, Kuda swimming behind her.

Aunt Scylla opened the door wider to let them in. "Say," she remarked, "didn't this door used to squeak?"

Lumina grinned. "It did. I fixed it," she announced proudly.

"Thank you, dear," Aunt Scylla said, smiling affectionately. "Always leaving things better than you found them." She patted Lumina on the arm. "I'll be in the kitchen. And I'm not even going to ask why there's a clamshell on Kuda's head."

Kuda's pink cheeks blushed red. "I appreciate that," she said.

As soon as Aunt Scylla turned her back, Lumina snatched the tiara off Kuda's head, sending a shower of pearls tumbling through the seawater.

Aunt Scylla whirled around. "Lumina!" she cried, seeing the shower of pearls. "Were you using your pearl magic outside?"

Lumina stared at her feet. "Um . . . well, maybe . . . just a little."

Scylla peered out into the yard, looking for anyone who might have witnessed Lumina's secret power. "Lumina, I've told you and told you: 'Keep your—'"

"'—magic to yourself,'" Lumina finished, trying not to roll her eyes. She had heard it a million times before.

Aunt Scylla sighed. "You have a very special gift, but if word got out, all kinds of bad people might come looking for you."

Lumina blew out her breath. "But I don't understand. Who's going to see me way out here?"

"You don't need to understand," her aunt snapped. "Please, just do as I say."

Lumina sighed. It was hard enough spending so much time alone, with only Kuda for company. She didn't think amusing herself with a few pearls could do any harm. Sure, it was an unusual talent to have. But Lumina had been able to control all the pearls around her for as long as she could remember. She used to wonder where her magical powers came from. Had her mother been able to command pearls? Her father? But she had stopped searching for answers a long time ago.

Her real parents were a mystery to her. The only family she had ever known was Aunt Scylla, who had adopted her when she was a baby. They'd lived in the sea cave, just the two of them, ever since. It was a nice, quiet life, and Lumina tried to be happy. But she couldn't help wondering what else might be out there for her.

Kuda brought Lumina back to reality with a grunt. "Great," the sea horse scoffed, rubbing her head where the clamshell crown had dug in. "Now your aunt's mad. And I've got clam dents in my head."

"Oh, you look fine," Lumina began. Then she squinted. "Except for your hair."

Kuda backed away. She recognized that glint in Lumina's eyes.

There was nothing Lumina loved more than creating things. Whether it was an elaborate throne in the front yard or a new hairstyle, she loved taking something ordinary and making it extraordinary. And she had to admit she was pretty good at it.

Lumina reached for Kuda's mane, a new style already in mind.

"Uh-oh." Kuda sighed.

Chapter 2

A short while later, after they had baked the kelp cake, Lumina got to work styling Kuda's mane. She added a few pearls. Then she took them out. Then she put them back in, rearranging them to frame Kuda's face. "Nope. Still not right."

She tried bangs. Then dreadlocks. Even a ballerina bun. But nothing seemed quite creative enough. Next, she spun Kuda's mane into an elaborate updo. She stepped back to admire her handiwork. "I think that's the one," she said, satisfied. "Now you need something to wear." She found a silk scarf in a drawer and draped it around Kuda like a gown. Using a starfish as a clip, she secured the gown in place. With a wave of her fingers she sprinkled it with pearls. "There. Now you look like a princess!"

Kuda spun around to face the mirror. "Only if a princess's hair is big enough to hold parties in!" she exclaimed, touching her mile-high do.

Lumina waved her arms, and a string of pearls whirled around her own golden hair, dressing it to match Kuda's. "Now we both look like princesses," she remarked, turning to admire her reflection from the side. She sighed. "I wonder what a real princess looks like."

❦

From her bedroom, Aunt Scylla listened sadly as Lumina and Kuda played dress-up. She picked up a pearl bracelet that had been Lumina's when she was a baby and felt the beads. She knew that, more than anything in the world, Lumina dreamed of being a princess, living in the royal castle and attending royal balls. She also knew that Lumina was, in fact, already a true princess.

Long ago—seventeen years, to be exact—Lumina was born in the royal castle. She was the only daughter of the king and queen of Seagundia—which made her Princess Lumina.

With flaxen hair and the gift of pearls, Princess Lumina would one day be queen herself. But while the town rejoiced, there was one member of the royal party who did not want her around.

Caligo, the king's brother-in-law, had another plan. He wished for his own son, Fergis, to inherit the throne. So Caligo hatched a villainous plot to get rid of Lumina.

Aunt Scylla was ashamed that she had kidnapped Lumina in exchange for payment from Caligo. But one look at Lumina's beautiful, smiling baby face and Scylla couldn't go through with the whole plan. So, to keep Lumina safe from Caligo's evil ways, Scylla raised her far away from the castle as her own niece—and loved her just as much as if she were.

Aunt Scylla shook her head free of the terrible memories. If only she could find some way to tell Lumina the truth. But every time she tried, she lost her nerve. She loved Lumina with all her heart, and telling her would only hurt her. Aunt Scylla replaced Lumina's pearl baby bracelet in her keepsake box and shut the lid tightly.

Across the sea at the royal palace, Caligo plotted once again for his son to rule the seas. It had been seventeen years since the princess disappeared, and he was getting impatient.

Since Lumina's disappearance, the king and queen had plunged into a deep sadness. They locked themselves away in the palace, refusing to see anyone or perform any of their royal duties. The kingdom missed their beloved king and queen.

Caligo didn't care whether the king and queen ever resumed their royal duties—just as long as they named Fergis the heir to the throne.

"Your Gracious Majesties, all I ask is that you consent to appear in public just one night. It's been seventeen long years. Your subjects need you. Your kingdom needs you. Dare I say it, I need you," Caligo pleaded in a slimy voice.

The king sighed a heavy sigh. "Caligo, I've told you many times. Queen Lorelei and I—"

Caligo put up a hand to stop the king. He pretended to wipe a tear from his eye. "Of course, of course, and like you, I am inconsolable with grief. But we simply must face the fact that with you and the queen having no heir, the kingdom will one day pass to your nephew—my gallant son, Fergis."

Shaggy-haired Fergis knelt in the corner, lovingly tending to a flower box of sea plants. He beamed goofily at his father and pointed to an exquisite bloom. "Look, Father, look!" he cried. "A Crinoidea *Porphyras*! The first one of the season! Oh, rapture! Wait until I tell the botany club."

Caligo rolled his eyes. Fergis was nothing like him. But he was Caligo's only shot at gaining all of the power that came with the royal throne. Whether Fergis wanted to or not, he would become king.

Caligo focused his attention once again on the king and queen. "Now that he has come of age, tradition dictates that we confer upon the heir apparent our royal medallion, the Pearl of the Sea." He eyed a glass case behind the royal couple. Inside the case lay a necklace with one enormous luminescent pearl hanging from it.

The queen fingered the locket she wore around her own neck, close to her heart. It held a picture of her lost baby girl. She nodded solemnly. "I'm afraid Caligo is right. Perhaps it is time."

The king nodded in agreement.

Caligo clapped his hands. "Excellent!" he cried, sounding a bit too excited. "And since he'll also need to choose a suitable wife, we'll give a royal ball. We'll invite the most eligible young mermaids of the kingdom—for a chance to be my son's queen!"

He glanced at Fergis, who was whispering to a blue sea lily. "Hello, *Neocrinus decorus*. How are you feeling today? A little blue? Ha, ha—get it?" He chuckled to himself.

The king rubbed his eyes. Fergis was not anyone's idea of a gallant prince. But he would have to do.

ChapteR 3

Aunt Scylla knitted her brows in concentration. She could hear Lumina and Kuda outside playing hide-and-seek as they looked for sea pearls. Carefully, Scylla poured a syrupy red liquid from one bamboo dish into another dish full of blue liquid. She had to get this latest scale-smoothing potion just right for a very high-maintenance client. Purple steam rose high into the air In the shape of a viperfish. Perfect. The steamy fish wound its way around a nearby houseplant, causing the plant to wither and die. *Looks like I still have some work to do,* Scylla thought.

Just then, she heard a knock on the door. She waved the steamy viperfish back into its crucible and quickly returned all of her ingredients to the cupboard. She opened the front door and peered out. Nobody was there. *That's strange,* she thought. Suddenly, an eel dangled in front of her face from the top of the doorway. He eyed her crazily.

"Ahhhhh!" Scylla cried in shock.

"Oh, my dear, did I frighten you?" the eel whispered menacingly. He let out a loud cackle.

"Who are you, and what do you want?" Scylla snapped.

The eel slithered along the doorframe, enjoying the suspense. "Murray at your service," he hissed, bowing deeply. "Merely a humble messenger. I come bearing an 'eel-mail' from an old friend of yours: Caligo."

Hearing Caligo's name, Scylla jumped back. She had tried so hard to put him—and her dreadful past—from her mind. "How did you find me here?" she asked.

"Oh, I have a certain gift for finding those who don't want to be found," Murray replied. He slinked past Scylla into the living room.

"Hey! Out!" Scylla commanded.

Murray ignored her. "I admit tracking you

down was a particular challenge. But my Bottom Feeders Network came through. Then it was simply a slither here, a slither there, and—voilà!—here I am." He swam under the couch just as Scylla tried to grab him.

"All right, you've found me," Scylla replied with a sigh. "What is it you want?"

Murray reappeared. "A simple request, really. My employer is once again in need of your, um, professional services."

Scylla's eyes narrowed. "Services? What services?"

"It seems Caligo has grown a bit impatient waiting for His Majesty the King to die of natural causes. He has decided, therefore, to speed up the process a tad," Murray announced darkly.

Scylla nodded, understanding. "Ahh, *those* services."

Murray slithered around her feet and tried to settle himself in a nearby chair. "Precisely. He has convinced His Majesty to open up the castle for a royal ball, at which time the king will confer the Pearl of the Sea medallion on Caligo's son.

His Majesty will then toast the boy with a cup of merberry nectar."

Scylla eyed Murray with suspicion. "Which Caligo wants me to poison," she concluded.

"Exactly," Murray replied, slinking out of the chair. "The king croaks, the son is crowned, everybody wins. . . . Well, maybe not the king. Don't you love a happy ending?"

Scylla had heard enough. "Well, you can tell your 'employer' that I'm no longer in the poisoning business. So unless you're interested in buying some Gill Glistener or Scale Brighter, GET OUT!" She pointed to the door.

Murray did not budge. "He said you'd say that," he hissed. "I am therefore authorized to issue the following threat: 'Do it, or I'll tell everyone you killed the princess.'"

Scylla gasped. "He wouldn't dare!" she whispered fiercely.

Murray flashed a sinister smile. "He said you'd say that, too. I am therefore authorized to respond: 'Would so.'"

Scylla's eyes blazed with fury. She had made

some mighty big mistakes in her life, but Caligo was truly evil. If he issued a threat, it was likely to come true. She couldn't risk putting Lumina in any sort of danger. Scylla had no choice. "Fine. If it's poison Caligo wants, it's poison he'll get."

"A wise decision," Murray remarked. "Here, you'll need this invitation to the ball. We'll leave the sordid details in your expert hands. After all, it's really all in the 'execution.' Wouldn't you agree?" The eel chuckled smugly as he swam toward the door. "Now don't be late—eight p.m., Saturday, at the castle."

Just then, Scylla heard another voice. "Castle?"

Lumina floated in through the open doorway. Scylla winced. Things were about to get complicated.

"What about the castle?" Lumina asked excitedly.

Murray flashed a curious grin. "Well, well, and who is this?" he hissed, swimming around Lumina to examine her.

"Hi!" Lumina said cheerfully. "I'm—"

Scylla cut her off. "—late for dinner! Our guest was just leaving." She pushed Murray toward the door.

"But, Aunt Scylla!" Lumina protested.

"Aunt Scylla?" Murray asked, raising an eyebrow. "I assumed you lived alone."

"You assumed wrong. Get out," Scylla ordered, shoving the eel through the door and slamming it in his face. She hoped he hadn't figured out who Lumina really was.

Chapter 4

"Aunt Scylla," Lumina said excitedly, "what was your friend talking about? Did he mean the royal castle? Are you going there? Can I go? Pleeeease?" Lumina could hardly contain her curiosity. After all, it wasn't every day that someone visited the sea cave and spoke of the royal palace. She had to know everything!

Aunt Scylla rubbed her temples.

Lumina could tell her aunt didn't want to talk about it, but she couldn't help herself. "I heard it has golden doors and pearl chandeliers and a beautiful throne! It must be wonderful, and I've always wanted to go there and so does Kuda and—"

"Stop!" Aunt Scylla interrupted. "Absolutely not! I've told you how dangerous the journey is!

I do it to sell my potions, but it's far too risky for a young girl alone."

"But I wouldn't be alone!" Lumina protested. "I'd have you! And Kuda!"

"And burning fire coral! And vampire squid! And poisonous stonefish!" Aunt Scylla said, shaking her head.

Lumina pouted. Kuda looked terrified.

Aunt Scylla softened. "Lumina, neither of you has ever been an inch outside this reef. Believe me; you wouldn't last two seconds, even with me to keep an eye on you."

"But—" Lumina tried.

"It's out of the question," Aunt Scylla declared, floating out of the room.

"I think that's a no," Kuda joked, trying to put a smile on Lumina's crestfallen face.

Lumina let out a miserable sigh. Why did everything interesting have to be off-limits? She longed to see the world beyond the reef. She wanted to travel, see sights she had only dreamed of. But Aunt Scylla thought she was safest at home. Where was the adventure in that?

The next morning, Lumina and Kuda watched glumly as Aunt Scylla packed for her trip to the palace. *Maybe if I look just sad enough, Aunt Scylla will take me with her,* Lumina thought.

But she was wrong. "You be good," her aunt instructed as she floated toward the door. "I'll be back in a few days. And please, both of you, stick close to home."

She kissed them good-bye and took off into the great, wide sea.

Lumina shut the door behind her and sighed. Now what?

"Want to play Tic-Tac-Tuna?" Kuda asked.

Lumina shook her head. She was too disappointed to do much of anything. Lost in thought, she straightened a stack of papers on a nearby table. "Hmm. What's this?" she asked. She picked up a large, glossy envelope and opened it. "It's an invitation!" she cried. "Aunt Scylla's not *just* going to the castle! She's invited to the royal ball!" Lumina read the details on the invitation. "And she can't get in without this!"

Lumina waved the invitation in the air. She raced to the door and flung it open. "Aunt Scylla!" she called. "You forgot your—" She looked both ways but her aunt was already gone. Suddenly, she got an idea. "Kuda," she began, a twinkle in her eye. "We really should bring this to Aunt Scylla, don't you think?"

"No, I don't think," Kuda replied, eyeing her warily.

But Lumina's face glowed with excitement. "But she'll need it to get into the ball. So when you think about it, it's really our duty to go after her—all the way to the castle if we have to!"

Kuda shook her head. "Were you listening to Aunt Scylla? Remember the dangerous journey?"

"You mean the burning whatsit and the poisonous thing-a-ma-poo?" Lumina replied, already making plans in her head.

"It was burning fire coral and poisonous stonefish and you know it," Kuda declared.

"What about the castle, and the king and queen, and the beautiful mermaids, and all the things we've always wanted to see?" Lumina said, practically singing with anticipation.

"But we were just playing!" Kuda protested. "I never thought we'd really do it!"

Lumina knelt in front of Kuda. "Don't you see?" she asked earnestly. "This is our big chance! Oh, Kuda, we've got to go! We've just got to!"

"But . . . ," Kuda started, even though she knew it had already been decided. There was nothing to do but go along to make sure Lumina stayed safe.

Chapter 5

A short while later, after they had packed only the essentials into Lumina's pearl purse, Kuda and Lumina set off through the sea.

"This has to be the right way," Lumina said, examining her surroundings. They swam through a colorful coral reef, passing schools of tropical fish and fields of anemones along the way. "I've seen Aunt Scylla head this way every time she goes to town."

Suddenly, Lumina stopped. Kuda bumped right into her. *Oof!* On the wall in front of them, red-orange fire coral rose as far as the eye could see.

"It's a dead end," Lumina stated.

"Darn," Kuda said, pretending to be disappointed. "We gave it our best. Let's go home."

But Lumina wasn't ready to give up. She examined the wall more closely, looking for some way around it. She noticed a tiny opening high above. "There!" she exclaimed.

"Where?" Kuda replied, not looking all that closely.

"That opening! I bet that's her shortcut through the coral," Lumina reasoned, swimming toward it.

"That? That's not an opening, that's a dot!" Kuda objected. "Not even a big dot! You couldn't push a guppy through there!"

Lumina reached the opening and squeezed her way in. It was just barely her size. "Follow me, Kuda! Don't be afraid!"

Reluctantly, Kuda followed Lumina's lead.

The friends entered a massive cavern covered with fragile fire coral. It was dark and dangerous, with giant slabs of coral hanging close to their heads.

"Slow down, Lumina!" Kuda begged. She smacked into a coral stalactite by accident. "Uh-oh!" It broke off and started a chain reaction. Coral rained down from the ceiling of the cavern.

"Kuda! Swim faster!" Lumina urged as the tunnel started to break apart around them. They made their way through the collapsing coral until—*crash!* A giant boulder of coral smashed to the ground right in front of them, blocking their path. Lumina and Kuda retreated, but the path back was jammed with coral, too.

Lumina tried not to panic. There had to be another way out. She looked around frantically and spotted a side tunnel. "In there!"

They plowed through the tunnel's narrow entry. Twisting and turning to dodge falling coral, Lumina coached Kuda. "Don't be afraid!" she called. "Swim faster! You can do it!"

With a final burst of speed, Kuda and Lumina lunged toward the opening at the other end of the tunnel. They swam through just as the tunnel collapsed behind them.

"That was fun!" Lumina cried, her eyes twinkling with delight.

"That was horrible," Kuda mumbled.

Soon they arrived at a forest of waving kelp. Lumina noticed a thin path winding through the tall, dimly lit seaweed. "This is it! I know it! See that path? We just need to follow it." She zoomed down the path, Kuda racing to catch up. They were so busy looking forward that they didn't notice two gleaming eyes peering at them from behind the kelp.

Meanwhile, at the castle, preparations were under way for the royal ball. Everyone was excited—except Fergis, the ball's honorary attendee. He wanted to stay at home with his plants. In fact, he wanted to skip this whole "inheriting the throne" business completely. But he also wanted to make his father proud. He wasn't sure how to do both.

"But, Father, do I have to go to the ball?" he whined.

"Yes, Fergis," Caligo replied impatiently. "The ball is being given for you. Once His Majesty places the Pearl of the Sea medallion on you, no power on earth can stop me—I mean, you—from someday being king."

Fergis pouted. "But I've told you—I don't want to be king. I want to be a botanist."

"And I've told you," Caligo thundered, glaring at Fergis, "you'll do what I say! You'll go to that ball, find a suitable wife, and be named the next ruler of Seagundia!"

Fergis wilted like a flower under his father's harsh words. "But I love plants, Father, I just love them," he said in a small voice. "I love all of them: the *Syringodium* and the *Rhizophora* and the cheeky little *Sargassum*." He smiled as he pictured a beautiful garden containing all of his favorites. He pulled a tiny flower bud from his pocket and sniffed it happily.

Caligo snatched the flower and threw it to the ground. "Forget about plants!" he ordered. "You're going to be king and that's the end of it, understood? Now get back to your waltz lessons."

Fergis sighed heavily. "Yes, sir," he mumbled, stooping to pick up the crushed bud his father had discarded. "Forgive me, *Sargassum,*" he whispered to it as he trudged out of the room.

Caligo rubbed his temples in frustration. He was so close to the throne he could taste it. He would not let his son's flowery dreams stand in the way of the power that rightly belonged to him. Lost in his thoughts, he didn't notice Murray slip into the room.

The eel cleared his throat, announcing his arrival.

"*Ahhhhh!* Don't do that!" Caligo cried, practically jumping out of his skin. He did not like surprises.

The eel chuckled. "I can't help myself."

"Well? Did you find Scylla?" Caligo asked impatiently.

"I did, and she agreed to do it," the eel hissed.

Caligo smiled nastily. "Excellent. Once she's poisoned the king at the ball, I will finish off Scylla." He drew his finger across his neck to illustrate his point. "I'll be hailed as a national hero, and my son will be crowned King of Seagundia."

"What if the guards grab her first?" Murray asked, poking a hole in Caligo's master plan.

"They won't," Caligo answered confidently. "The Trident Squad is loyal only to me. And I've arranged that they will be the ones guarding the ballroom."

Murray nodded in approval. "My, you have thought of everything."

"I make it my business to. And once my son is king, I will hold the real power in the kingdom." He rubbed his hands together greedily. Reaching into his desk, he retrieved a small sack of gold coins. He tossed the payment to Murray for a job well done and looked at a picture of Fergis on his desk. "Now comes the hard part," he continued. "Finding someone to marry Fergis."

Murray slithered toward the door. "Perhaps you should talk to Scylla," he said slyly. "You know, she has quite a lovely niece."

Caligo yanked Murray back into the room by his tail. "Niece?" he asked.

"Goodness me," Murray said, acting innocent. "Did I fail to mention that? Blond, about seventeen years old. Interesting coincidence, don't you think?"

Caligo dropped Murray and stroked his chin in thought. "Hmmm." Seventeen years ago he'd hired Scylla to make that blond baby princess disappear. Could this be the same mergirl? He eyed Murray dangerously. "Bring me that niece. I want to ask her a few questions."

Chapter 6

Lumina weaved her way through the narrow pathway of kelp, Kuda behind her. A pair of yellow eyes watched them, unnoticed.

"This forest goes on forever," Kuda commented. "And it's getting kind of dark. Can't we go back now? My fins are tired."

Lumina peered through the sea grass in front of her and saw lights in the distance. "Lights!" she cried. "Could that be the city already?" She picked up her pace and strayed from the path to check it out.

Kuda gulped. Leaving the path did not seem like a smart idea.

Lumina raced toward a clearing. She screeched to a halt when she saw giant squid floating in front of her. Their red eyes glowed in the deep dark water and their cloak-like tentacles reached toward Lumina.

"This can't be as bad as it looks," Lumina said, not wanting to scare Kuda.

But Kuda, hiding behind her, was already terrified. "It's worse! Those are vampire squid!"

Lumina gulped. "Well, I'm sure if we don't bother them, they won't bother us."

The vampire squid moved closer.

"Tell that to *them*!" Kuda cried.

Slowly, Lumina and Kuda tried to back away. But the vampire squid had them trapped on three sides! The squid opened their gaping mouths, and Lumina saw what looked like sharp teeth inside.

Kuda grabbed a nearby stick with her tail. "Well, I'm not going down without a fight!" she cried, waving the stick in front of her.

Suddenly, the squid stopped in their tracks.

"Wow, nice going, Kuda!" Lumina cheered.

Kuda looked proud. "I guess they knew better than to mess with us!" She shuffled back and forth like a boxer. "Float like a butterflyfish, sting like a jelly wasp!" she cried.

Then Lumina realized that the squid were staring at something behind them. Uh-oh. She whirled around and screamed, *"Whooooaaa!"*

A giant vampire squid the size of a boat drifted toward them. Its huge underside glowed a ghastly blue.

Thinking quickly, Lumina reached into her pouch. She threw fistful after fistful of pearls toward the giant squid.

"I don't think it's pearls he wants to eat!" Kuda exclaimed.

Lumina ignored her friend and commanded the pearls to form the outline of an enormous eye against the boulder behind them. It made the boulder look like a sea monster twice the size of the vampire squid. Lumina conducted the "eye" to glare dangerously. The giant squid swam away in terror! Score!

Kuda grinned. "Not bad!" Then she frowned. "Uh-oh."

Lumina groaned. "Stop saying that!'"

Kuda's eyes widened with fear. "Move. Away.

From the rock," she ordered.

"Why?" Lumina asked, still feeling great about defeating the vampire squid.

The boulder behind her sprang to life. It wasn't a rock at all but a giant stonefish! And it was angry. *ROOOOAAARRRR!* Its cry thundered through the sea.

"That's why!" Kuda cried, shaking. "A stonefish! One of the most poisonous—"

"The *most* poisonous!" the stonefish bellowed, his voice shaking the water around them.

Kuda cleared her throat quietly. "Make that the most poisonous fish in the sea," she said in a tiny voice.

"That's right, mergirl! You are looking at the face of certain doom!" the fish shouted.

Lumina took a deep breath. She held out her hand to greet the menacing fish. "Uh, nice to meet you, Mr. Doom," she tried.

"So you better move it! *ROOAAARRR!*" the stonefish shouted.

"I vote with him," Kuda said, spinning to

leave. "Let's do what he says."

Lumina grabbed Kuda by the tail. "Hang on."

"I said, *ROOAARR!*" the stonefish tried once more.

Lumina cocked her head thoughtfully. Something about this stonefish caught her attention. He seemed almost sad. "That is one powerful voice you have there," she remarked.

The stonefish charged toward Lumina. She felt his hot breath on her face as he glared at her.

"Aren't you listening?" he yelled. Then he pointed to the thirteen sharp spikes along the ridge of his back. "You see these spikes? They're poisonous! One prick and game over. Kaput! You're finished."

But Lumina wasn't fazed. She knew her pearl powers could render his spikes useless. Besides, she wanted the chance to talk to him more—to find out what made him so angry. So she waved her hand and thirteen large pearls zipped out of her pouch. They darted through the water and landed, one atop each of the stonefish's sharp spikes. "There," Lumina said.

The stonefish eyed his back. "What?" he bellowed. "What have you done to me?"

Kuda ducked behind Lumina for safety. "Y-y-yeah," she stammered. "What have you done to him?"

"I just de-spiked your spikes," Lumina replied matter-of-factly. "Now no one needs to be scared of you."

The stonefish looked worried. "What? Nooo! You can't do this! I'm the scariest thing in the ocean!" He thrashed around and let out a deafening roar to prove his point.

Kuda peeked from behind Lumina. Something about a huge fish covered in pearls didn't seem so scary after all. "Not so much the scariest. Just the loudest," the sea horse ventured.

The stonefish looked miserable—as if he wasn't sure how to act without his weapons. "Great. Just great. What am I supposed to do now?" he asked, deflated.

Lumina swam closer. "Just be nicer," she suggested. "Stop trying to frighten everyone.

Get to know your fellow fish."

"Easy for *you* to say." The stonefish pouted, sinking into the sand. "Everyone runs from me."

Lumina sat beside him and patted his fin gently. She hated to see anyone—even a big scary stonefish—feel lonely and left out. Having spent so much time by herself at the sea cave, she knew what it felt like. "Well, I think you should give the pearls a chance. Once no one's afraid of you, I bet you'll have loads of friends," she said sweetly.

The stonefish considered Lumina's words. "You think? I don't know. It seems wrong for a stonefish. And I'm not so good at friendliness."

Lumina waved her hand through the air, sweeping the stonefish's concerns away. "We're heading to the city. There's lots of fish there, Mr. Doom. And you could practice being friendly to them."

"The name's Spike," the stonefish replied, showing a hint of a smile. "You don't mind if I come along?"

Lumina rose and held out her hand toward

Spike. "I'd be honored," she said with a curtsey.

Kuda inched her way toward Spike. "And I'd be more nervous than honored," she half joked, offering her tail. "But I'll give it a shot."

The three new friends joined fins and took off through the wide-open sea.

Chapter 7

As Lumina headed toward the city, Murray snaked his way through the kelp forest to her sea cave. He carried a coil of rope and a mermaid-size sack. When he arrived, he knocked on the front door. *Rap. Rap. Rap.* "Candy-gram!" he shouted in his best girly voice.

No answer.

He knocked again, louder this time. "Bob the Birthday Squid!" he tried.

Still no answer.

RAP. RAP. RAP. RAP. "Eel Scout Cookies!" he called. "Collecting for Snails Without Tails!"

Where is that girl? he thought impatiently. He peeked through the open window. Nobody home. He slithered inside and inspected each room. In the kitchen, he found a note Lumina had written. He read it aloud. " 'Aunt Scylla—You left behind your ball invitation, so we're bringing it to you. See you at the castle. Love, Lumina.' "

With his tail, Murray crumpled up the note in frustration. "Victims! Never there when you need them," he mumbled grumpily. He poked around the room, looking for something—anything—to make his journey worthwhile. Nothing! He zoomed into Scylla's room next. "As long as I'm here . . . ," he reasoned.

He nosed around Scylla's dresser, looking at her various knickknacks. Then he spotted a keepsake box covered in seashells. He opened it with the tip of his tail and peered in. "Oh," he gasped, admiring a small pearl baby bracelet at the bottom of the box. He picked it up to examine it more closely and flashed an evil grin. The bracelet carried the royal seal.

He'd found the proof. Now all he needed was the girl.

Lumina, Kuda, and Spike wound their way farther through the dense kelp, cracking jokes along the way. *It's nice,* Lumina thought, *to have a new friend along.*

Suddenly, Kuda got snagged in a bit of kelp that seemed to come alive and trap her!

"Huh?" Kuda cried, surprised. "Help! Kelp! Help! Kelp!"

"Whoa!" Spike cried, lunging toward Kuda. "She swam right into a bed of SnarlyKelp! That stuff never lets go!"

Lumina and Spike struggled to free their sea horse friend, but the kelp tried to grab them, too. Lumina bobbed and weaved, ducking out of the SnarlyKelp's reach.

"Spike, quick! If I uncap one of your spikes, do you think you could use the point to cut Kuda loose without stabbing or poisoning her?" Lumina asked.

Spike bit his lip, unsure. "Maybe," he said. "There's a first time for everything."

Lumina nodded. She waved her hands and a large pearl popped off one of the stonefish's spikes. "Be careful," she said.

Spike swam underneath Kuda and tried to sever the SnarlyKelp strands without touching the sea horse.

Kuda's eyes grew big with panic. "Hey, wait!" she cried. "Isn't there another way?" She struggled to move away from Spike.

"Hold still!" Spike pleaded. "You've got to hold still!"

As Kuda forced herself to remain calm and still, Spike carefully jabbed at the last strand of SnarlyKelp. *Snap!*

Kuda broke free. "Thanks, Spike. Okay, that's it. I've had it. I'm going home. Scylla was right. We'll never make it in one piece to the—" Kuda stopped speaking when she noticed Lumina and Spike grinning goofily at something behind her.

Kuda turned around slowly to see a stunning, glittering mermaid city. In the center of the skyline, the royal castle sparkled. They'd made it!

Overjoyed, Lumina floated down the hill, toward the bustling, brilliant streets. In all the commotion, she didn't notice that her aunt's invitation to the ball had fallen out of her pouch.

Lumina couldn't believe her eyes. Seagundia was even more beautiful than it had been in her dreams. The city's tall floating buildings were decorated with scalloped doorways and starfish topiaries. Its avenues teemed with merfolk riding in gilded carriages pulled by orca whales. Street vendors sold delicacies from turtle-shell pushcarts.

It all took Lumina's breath away. "Wow." She sighed and looked at her dumbstruck friends with a smile. She knew that with time, they would love this city as much as she already did.

Honk! Honk! Just then, a two-orca carriage came speeding up behind them. Its merman driver honked his blowfish horn at them. "Hey, out of my way!" he shouted.

"Sorry!" Lumina replied as she darted from his path just in time and bumped into a passerby. "Excuse me!"

"Everyone is in such a hurry," Kuda said.

Lumina nodded and glanced at Spike, who was still skulking along in the shadows. She knew he felt nervous about how merfolk might react to seeing a stonefish on their city streets. "Spike, why are you hiding? You have nothing to worry about," she reminded him.

"Okay," Spike replied unsurely. He stepped out into the sunlit street. "The screaming usually kicks in about now." He cringed, waiting.

But instead of screaming, a nearby mermaid approached him. "Love your pearls," she said.

Spike grinned in surprise. "You do?"

"Oh, yeah," another mermaid added. "Great look!"

Before long a crowd of admirers had gathered around Spike.

"So cool!"

"Let me see!"

"Who does your spikes?"

Spike fluttered his eyelashes and basked in all the attention. It was amazing. Lumina beamed with pride. She loved helping a friend feel confident.

"Talk about an extreme makeover!" Kuda exclaimed. Then something farther down the street caught her eye. "Lumina, look!" she cried.

Lumina cast a glance down the road and grinned. Aunt Scylla was walking out of a shop! She had her head down, searching for something in her bag.

"It's Scylla!" Kuda confirmed. "Have you got her invitation?"

Lumina rummaged through her pouch, but the invitation was nowhere to be found. "It's gone! I must have lost it on the way!"

"What?" Kuda cried, nervously swimming around in circles. "She is never going to believe us. She'll be angry we left the reef!"

Lumina cringed. Kuda had a point. "Well," she said, recovering, "I'll just explain that we were trying to help out and—"

"—and you'll be grounded for a year!" Kuda interrupted. "Come on!" The sea horse zipped off, dragging Lumina by her tail.

They dashed down an alley, checking behind them to make sure Scylla hadn't spotted them yet. Kuda eyed a doorway nearby and motioned toward it.

"Wait," Lumina whispered urgently. "What about Spike?"

They looked back to see Spike surrounded by admirers.

"He's doing fine!" Kuda replied. "Quick! In here!"

They ducked through the door and slammed it shut.

Lumina leaned against the door to catch her breath.

"Whew!" Kuda sighed with relief.

Just then, a large, billowy orange octopus with a fancy hairdo bustled toward them.

"Oh, thank goodness!" the octopus cried, sweeping her hair out of her face.

Lumina and Kuda exchanged a look. Huh?

The octopus grabbed Lumina by the arm and dragged her through a curtain. Kuda followed them.

In the next room, Lumina saw a busy beauty salon. Merfolk sat, having their hair done and their faces made up. The walls echoed with their chatter. Lumina heard music playing in the background and noticed photos on the walls of glamorous mermaids modeling gorgeous hairdos. The room was lined with pink and purple drapes. *What a fun place to work,* Lumina thought.

"This way, sweetie," the octopus clucked. "I'll get you all set up!"

Lumina paused. "But I . . . ," she started. Obviously this octopus—lovely as she was—had mistaken Lumina for someone else. She had to explain.

But the octopus didn't seem to have heard Lumina. She whisked her by various styling stations for hair, nails, and makeup. There was even a whirlpool for spa treatments!

"So, do you have references? Do you have a résumé? Do you have a hairpin? My bun's coming undone!" The octopus fired questions at Lumina, making her head spin.

They passed a customer sitting in a chair shaped like a seashell. "Madame Ruckus!" The customer beckoned to the orange octopus. "Are you sure this blush is right for the royal ball?"

She examined her cheeks in a hand mirror.

Madame Ruckus swirled the customer's chair around. "Trust me, honey," she cooed. "That color is you!" Then she returned her attention to Lumina, hustling her into a styling station by the front window. "Now, let's see what you can do!" she announced.

Chapter 8

As Lumina wondered what to do, the salon phone rang and the octopus lunged for it. "Salon La Mer! Madame Ruckus speaking. You bet, ma'am, we can squeeze you in before the ball—four o'clock tomorrow?" She penciled something in an appointment book with one tentacle. She used a second tentacle to apply more blush to a customer and two more to sweep hair from the floor and help a teenage mermaid pick a style from a glossy magazine.

Eight arms sure come in handy in this place, Lumina mused.

"Madame Ruckus!" another customer called.

"Hang on, honey," she replied. "I can only do eight things at once!"

All this activity made Lumina dizzy—in a good

way. Sure, she had styled Kuda's mane hundreds of times, but it had always been just for fun. She couldn't imagine being an actual stylist, creating new looks every day in such a busy and exciting place.

Just then, Kuda tugged on her arm and pointed out the front window. "Scylla's coming!" the sea horse warned. "Quick—disguise hair!"

Lumina gasped as she saw her aunt heading down the street—right toward the salon! Faster than a flying fish, she directed the pearls in her hair. They twisted her locks into a peekaboo hairstyle, covering half her face.

Freaking out, Kuda grabbed a nearby wig and slapped it crookedly on her head.

The friends stood perfectly still as Scylla paused and peered into the salon window. She looked closely at Kuda and Lumina for a long moment, but then she kept walking.

Kuda nearly fainted with relief. "Whoa, that was close!" she said.

Madame Ruckus hung up her phone and spun to face Lumina. Her mouth dropped open in shock when she saw Lumina's elaborate new hairdo. "Wow!" she exclaimed. "You got the job!"

Lumina grinned. "A job?" she repeated in disbelief. "I have a job?" The more she said it, the more excited she got. If she worked at Salon La Mer she could be a part of the hustle and bustle every day! No more time spent by herself, with only Kuda for company. Plus, she would get to do what she loved: she could use her creativity to help people look their best and live life to the fullest. She could help people feel confident and happy—just like she'd done for Spike. But what would Aunt Scylla say?

She didn't have time to think about it, because the next thing she knew, Madame Ruckus ushered over the teen mergirl she'd helped sort through magazines. She plopped her down in the styling chair in front of Lumina.

"Here's your first customer!" she announced, waving a tentacle dramatically through the air. "Lunch break's at noon. We close at five. By the way, what's your name, hon?" She rushed off without waiting for an answer.

"Lumina!" Lumina called after her.

"Okay, Scylla's gone," Kuda said, ditching the wig. "Let's get out of here."

Lumina looked at the teen waiting expectantly in her chair. "I have a customer," she said.

Kuda rolled her eyes. "Remember the royal castle? The reason we came here in the first place?"

Lumina frowned. "You're right," she said, running her fingers through the teen's limp hair. "But she needs me. Just look."

The teen mermaid looked offended.

"We'll leave right after this, Kuda," Lumina promised. "Isn't it exciting? My first job!"

Kuda sighed. Once Lumina had made up her mind, there was no use arguing. She helped fasten a styling cape around the girl, and Lumina busily got to work.

The stylist at the next station leaned over. "So you're the new stylist, huh?" she said. Lumina nodded. "Well, newbie, I got two rules: keep your hand out of my tip jar, and don't ever touch my lucky brush. Okay?" She held up a beautiful silver-handled hairbrush.

Lumina bit her lip. "Sure, I guess," she said uncertainly. It seemed that not everyone at Salon La Mer was as friendly as Madame Ruckus.

"Don't let her scare you, honey!" Madame Ruckus called to Lumina from across the room. "That's Sandrine—she's half barracuda." Then the octopus pointed to another stylist. "And this is Cora. She does nails and tails," she explained.

Cora gave a friendly wave from across the salon.

Lumina relaxed a little.

"Can you do my hair like her?" Lumina's teen customer asked. She held up a picture ripped from a magazine.

Lumina examined the picture. "Well, I can if you want. But you know what might look even better—"

"I want to look like her!" the girl whined.

Sandrine leaned over and whispered in Lumina's ear. "Piece of advice, newbie: just give them what they want. Trust me; they're all wearing the same hairstyle."

Lumina sighed and continued combing the girl's hair. "Hmm," she mumbled to herself. Then she got an idea. She spun the girl away from the mirror and grabbed a fistful of pearls from her pouch.

"Lumina, no!" Kuda cried, realizing that Lumina was about to take matters into her own hands. She did it to Kuda all the time, but this was a paying customer. Lumina could get in trouble!

Lumina ignored her friend—she had a plan. She tossed the pearls into the air and conducted them to lift and shape the girl's hair into a magnificent modern style. She dotted the girl's new, soft waves with pearls and paused to think. "Let me see your eyes," she said, bending down to look. She changed the pearls' color to match the girl's lovely green eyes. Then she whirled the chair around again to show her client her handiwork.

Kuda held her breath in fear.

"Hey!" the girl gasped, her mouth dropping

open in shock. But her shock soon turned to glee. "That is *SO. TOTALLY. AWESOME!*" she cried, turning to admire her new look from every angle.

Lumina beamed proudly. "I knew you'd like it," she told the girl.

"Like it? I love it!" the girl cried, bursting with excitement. She stood up so everyone in the salon could see her.

The salon exploded with compliments, and the girl blushed happily. Then she rushed out the door to show her friends.

"Okay," Kuda conceded. "You got lucky— nobody saw that. Now can we go?"

Lumina grinned. "Next!" she called.

Another teen mermaid plopped down in Lumina's chair. "I want my hair just like you did hers!" she announced.

"Are you sure?" Lumina asked. "How about something special—just for you?"

"Really?" the girl squealed.

Lumina nodded and grabbed another handful of pearls.

CHAPTER 9

Back at the castle, Caligo met the ten-soldier Trident Squad in a dark underground passage. The squad carried dangerous trident weapons and wore special shoulder patches to set them apart from the rest of the royal guard.

"Have you briefed the men about the ball?" Caligo asked the Trident captain. Everything had to go as planned for Caligo to seize the throne and get rid of Scylla.

"Yes, sir," the captain replied. "Don't worry—they know exactly what to do."

Caligo smirked. "Splendid. I'll meet you back at the barracks," he said.

Just then, Scylla stepped out of the shadows to greet him.

"Everything is arranged," Caligo explained.

"The rest is up to you."

"I'll have access to the king?" Scylla asked.

"Yes," Caligo replied. "The royal beverage steward has taken ill." He gave Scylla an evil wink and gestured for her to follow him down the hall.

They worked their way toward the servers' quarters behind the grand ballroom and entered the beverage closet. Inside, bottles of all shapes and sizes lined the fancy wrought-iron shelves.

"You will take the steward's place at the ball and serve mulberry nectar to the royal party—including His Majesty," Caligo explained. He pointed to a set of goblets and an empty pitcher on a giant silver serving tray.

Scylla nodded. All she needed to do was add a few drops of poison to the king's goblet and their plan would be complete.

"The king will present the Pearl of the Sea to my son, then drink the toast. Then be gone forever," Caligo said darkly.

"I have the ingredients," Scylla told him. "But I'll need time to brew the poison."

Lumina uses her pearl magic
with her friend Kuda.

Murray the eel delivers a special message
for Lumina's aunt Scylla.

Lumina and Kuda set out
for the kingdom of Seagundia.

Lumina pearlizes Spike the stonefish's
poisonous spikes.

Lumina, Kuda, and Spike arrive
in Seagundia.

Lumina meets Madame Ruckus
at Salon La Mer.

Lumina loves her new job!

Caligo hatches an evil plan.

Lumina and her friends get ready
for the royal ball.

Lumina makes a grand entrance.

Lumina overhears Caligo's evil plot.

Caligo tries to stop Scylla
from telling the truth.

Lumina tries to stop Caligo
from poisoning the king.

Thanks to Fergis, Lumina is able
to save Scylla!

Lumina stops Caligo for good.

Lumina discovers that she is
the princess of Seagundia!

Caligo smiled menacingly. "You rid me of one pest seventeen years ago—now you'll rid me of another. Needless to say, you will be suitably rewarded."

Scylla pulled her hooded cloak over her face and turned to exit.

"Oh, by the way," Caligo said casually. "I understand you have a niece."

"What of it?" Scylla scoffed, trying to hide her unease. How did Caligo know about Lumina? And worse, did he suspect that Lumina was the very same princess she'd kidnapped all those years ago?

Caligo smiled. "Please give her my regards," he said.

Scylla shivered at Caligo's threatening tone and hurried on her way. Only time would tell just how much danger she—and Lumina—were in. She vowed to be prepared.

The next day, Lumina worked hard on her third client at Salon La Mer. "What color gown are you wearing to the ball?" she asked.

"Hot pink with teal accents," the girl replied.

Lumina just waved her arms and—*ping!*—
the pearl accents she'd added to the girl's hair
turned teal. She spun the girl around to face the
mirror.

"This is amazing!" the girl said, gasping with
delight.

Another teen mermaid bounded through
the door. She ran toward Sandrine. "Are you
Lumina?" she asked.

Sandrine rolled her eyes and pointed toward
Lumina's station. "Next chair over. Better get in
line," she said grumpily, pointing to the long line
of mermaids waiting for a turn in Lumina's chair.
"She's only been here two days and everyone
thinks she invented hair."

"Oh dear, Kuda," Lumina said. We're going
to need a lot more pearls!"

🐚

Meanwhile, Caligo banged his fist against his
office desk. "Gone? What do you mean?"

Murray floated around the room and explained his visit to the sea cave again. "Gone. Vanished. Now she's here, now she's not. The place was empty."

Caligo looked out the window. "Blast! Someone must have tipped her off."

"I don't think so," Murray reasoned. "She left a note saying she was coming to the city. And I found this." He dangled Lumina's baby bracelet from his tail.

Caligo snatched it and examined it closely. "The royal crest!" he exclaimed. "Then it is her! That old mermaid double-crossed me! The princess is alive!"

Murray gave a sly grin. "The king and queen will be thrilled."

Caligo clenched his fist around the bracelet, practically crushing its beads. The princess complicated his plan considerably. The fact that she was alive meant that she—not Fergis—was the rightful heir to the throne. "This could ruin everything! We've got to get rid of her. Search everywhere! Get all your slimiest, sleaziest, creepiest cronies together."

"Not a problem," Murray responded. "That's the only kind I know."

Caligo's eyes blazed. "Find. That. Girl," he commanded.

Back at the salon, Lumina and the other stylists worked quickly. Word had spread about the exciting new styles coming out of Salon La Mer, and it seemed everyone wanted an appointment. They were so busy, they had even run out of supplies.

Just then, Madame Ruckus came bustling through the back door, holding armfuls of boxes.

New supplies—yes! Lumina thought. Then she noticed a handsome merman trailing behind Madame Ruckus. He carried another armload of boxes. A dolphin friend accompanied him.

"Excuse me, ma'am," he said from behind his load. "Perhaps you could be of some assistance. I'm afraid we're a bit lost."

But Madame Ruckus didn't hear him. "Thanks.

You're a doll. Just plop those boxes right here, and I'll grab some more." She breezed back outside.

"Of course," the merman said, practically dropping the boxes on the floor. *"Oof!"*

"Oh, good. Delivery is here," Sandrine said, tearing open one of the boxes and grabbing some hairspray.

Lumina swam over and smiled. "Did you bring some styling gel?" she asked politely.

"Styling gel?" the merman replied.

Lumina opened a box and grabbed a bottle. "Here it is."

"I'm sorry. I'm afraid I'm a bit new to this," the merman said, smiling sheepishly.

"It's okay. This is my first job, too. I'm Lumina," she said.

"Pleasure to meet you, Lumina. I'm Delphin," the merman replied.

"Dolphin?" Lumina asked, unsure that she'd heard him right.

"No, Delphin. Don't worry, I get that a lot," the merman replied, chuckling.

"Come on," his dolphin friend clicked. "We're late! We were supposed to be at the palace an hour ago."

Delphin nodded. "I hope to see you again!" he called to Lumina as he raced toward the door.

"Handsome!" Cora whispered to Lumina as Delphin exited.

"Well, aren't you the lucky one," Sandrine said.

Lumina blushed.

Madame Ruckus burst through the door with another round of boxes. She deposited them on the floor and whirled around with excitement. "Ladies! Hold on to your hairpins!" she cried. "I've got delightful news! I just ran into a dear old friend on the royal staff, and guess what she gave me?" She waved a piece of paper in the air.

"An invitation?" guessed Cora.

"To the royal ball?" cried Lumina.

"Tonight?" Sandrine asked.

Madame Ruckus clapped all eight of her tentacles. "For the whole staff!" she shouted, bubbling over with delight.

Lumina, Cora, and Sandrine jumped up and down, dancing together in a circle. Lumina could hardly believe her good fortune. Spending time preparing other mermaids for the special event had made her long even more to be a part of it all. Here was her chance!

Suddenly, Cora and Sandrine stopped dancing and looked serious.

"What are we going to wear?" they asked.

CHAPTER 10

A short while later, Murray slithered into a nearby alleyway. He peered into a Dumpster and spied his two cronies, Wormwood and Garth. If anyone could track down Lumina, it was these two. They weren't the brightest eels in the sea, but they could follow instructions.

"Hi, Boss!" Garth hissed in a goofy voice. "We were just having lunch."

"Charming," Murray sneered, turning up his nose at the smell. "Any sign of the princess yet?"

"We already found fifty girls who match her picture," Wormwood announced.

"What picture?" Murray responded.

Garth whipped out a baby picture of the princess and proudly showed his boss. "It's the only one we could find. She's drooling, but isn't she just adorable?" he asked.

Murray felt his face redden with anger. "You've been looking for babies?" He didn't bother explaining that the princess they were looking for was now seventeen years old.

Garth nodded dumbly as Wormwood said, "Don't worry, Boss. We brought them all to Caligo."

Murray froze with fear at the thought of his boss surrounded by dozens of babies. Caligo would certainly blame him. He gulped. Was that Caligo's voice he heard on the tide?

"Murray!"

He drew his knucklehead friends a more recent picture and dashed to clean up their mess.

❀

At noon, Lumina, Kuda, Cora, Sandrine, and Madame Ruckus talked and laughed as they made their way down the street to go shopping for the ball. They entered a clothing shop with two giant gargoyles by its doorway.

Inside the store, Madame Ruckus bounced about with enthusiasm. She fluttered over to Lumina and the girls, wearing a sparkling bangle bracelet.

"Look what I found, girls!" she cried. "Don't you love what this sparkle does for my tentacles? I'd better buy seven more," she continued, floating away.

Lumina flipped through a rack of drab-looking dresses and frowned. It didn't look like they had much to choose from.

"There's not much left, huh?" said Cora, echoing Lumina's thoughts.

"Nothing I'd wear to a ball," Sandrine agreed. "I guess the good gowns sold out long ago."

Lumina furrowed her brow and took another look through the rack. Her imagination kicked into high gear, and she smiled. "Oh, I don't know," she started. "I think we could do a lot with what's here. Add some ribbons, a little ruching, a little rickrack, and—presto!—our very own original styles!"

Cora clapped her hands together. "You really

think so?" she asked hopefully.

Lumina beamed. "Absolutely! And it'll be fun, too!"

Sandrine raised an eyebrow. "Fun?" she questioned.

Lumina plucked a plain pink dress from the rack. She spun around, holding it up to herself in the full-length mirror. "Like this," she stated. "I love this color. I could do all kinds of things to spice it up."

Cora touched a corner of the dress, admiring it. "Ooh, I didn't see this one. You're right—that pink is epic!"

Lumina held the dress against Cora, smiling warmly. "You know what? It's an even better color for you. You take it," she said, offering the dress to Cora.

"What?" Cora said, startled by Lumina's kindness. "Oh, no, I couldn't. You saw it first."

"But it's going to look so amazing on you! Here, take it. Please," Lumina insisted.

"Are you sure?"

Lumina nodded.

"Wow, thank you!" Cora cried, bounding off joyfully to try on the dress.

Sandrine crossed her arms and stared at Lumina. "Are you for real? That was the last dress in your size in the store! And the color was perfect for you. You said so yourself."

"It's okay, really," Lumina replied cheerfully. "I'm certain I'll find another one." She swam off in search of another dress.

Sandrine shook her head in disbelief. "It's sure not what I would have done," she mumbled.

Kuda swam up behind her. "But it's what Lumina does," she remarked proudly.

As the girls shopped, Wormwood and Garth waited outside. They had trailed Lumina all the way to the store and were about to put their plan in motion. Wormwood shook out a large, mermaid-size sack. They zipped around to the shop's front entrance and coiled themselves around the gargoyles. Now all they had to do was wait.

"Got everything I need—and a little more!" Madame Ruckus sang, holding eight armfuls of shopping bags. "See you back at the salon, ladies!"

She swam out the door—and right into Wormwood and Garth's trap! "Now!" Garth yelled.

They yanked the sack down over the octopus in one quick motion.

"Got her!" Wormwood replied.

They cinched the bag closed and tried to tow it away.

"Man, she's heavier than she looks," Garth said when he saw the picture Murray had drawn for them.

As they hauled the sack down the street, Madame Ruckus poked one, then two tentacles out of the opening. She tapped the eels on the shoulder.

Wormwood and Garth turned around. "Huh?"

Madame Ruckus slapped them with her tentacles, causing them to drop the sack. She escaped from the bag angrily and continued smacking the eels. "What do you think you're doing, you slimy little worms? I'll use you to floss my teeth!"

"Oh! *Oof!* Mercy!" the bumbling eels cried, struggling to get out of Madame's way.

But it was no use. Madame Ruckus was furious. She dragged the eels to a nearby lamppost and tied them to it. *That will teach them to mess with a lady,* she thought. She dusted off her tentacles, collected her bags, and swam away.

Lumina and Kuda swam over to the boutique's accessories counter, where they ran into Spike the stonefish. He still had pearls on his spikes and was checking out some scarves.

"Hi, guys!" he exclaimed. "Say, can you help me pick out a scarf for the ball?"

"Spike! You're going to the ball, too?" Kuda asked.

Spike puffed out his chest proudly. "Since Lumina pearlized me, I'm getting invited everywhere!" he explained.

Lumina picked up a hat from a nearby table. "This color might look nice with your spikes," she suggested.

Spike left the scarf display and tried on Lumina's hat. "I just realized I don't have a neck. So maybe a nice hat will do."

Just then, Lumina heard the town clock strike one.

"It's getting late," Kuda warned. "We'd better get going if you want to find another dress."

Lumina and her friends waved good-bye to Spike and headed down the street, peering into shop windows for more ball gowns. All around them, the streets of Seagundia were bustling with activity.

"I don't know where else to suggest," Cora said worriedly. "Seems like there's not another ball gown left in the kingdom."

Lumina waved away Cora's worries. "Don't worry, I'll figure something out for tonight."

As they crossed the street, two rough-looking eels jumped in front of them with a large empty sack. "Aha!" they shouted.

But suddenly, a fancy gold carriage pulled by two orca whales came hurtling down the street. *Bump!* It smacked right into the two eels, sending them flying.

"*Yaaaaaaoo!*" they cried as they landed on the other side of the street.

Lumina shook her head. So much activity today!

"This neighborhood's getting weird," Sandrine said.

❧

Inside their golden two-orca carriage, Fergis looked out the window, concerned. "Father," he asked, turning to Caligo in the seat beside him. "Did we just hit some pedestrians?"

"Who knows? Probably," Caligo responded. "Let's just get you to the tailor's. For one night, you need to look a little less like you. Then you've got a hair appointment—with the trendy new stylist at Madame Ruckus's salon."

Chapter 11

After their lunchtime shopping trip, Lumina returned to work at Salon La Mer. She fashioned a librarian's hair to look like an open, pearl-studded book!

"It's wonderful!" the librarian gasped. "I can't wait to show everyone back at the library!"

Lumina beamed and then reorganized her station for her next customer. Being the "it" hairstylist sure was exhausting! "Has anyone seen my brush?" she asked.

Sandrine held out her silver-handled hairbrush. "Here. Use mine," she offered.

Lumina was touched. "But isn't this your lucky hairbrush?" she asked.

Sandrine waved her hand through the air. "Don't make a big deal out of it," she grumbled.

Lumina grinned. With energy renewed, she waited for her next client to arrive.

Just then, the chime above the salon's front door tinkled. Caligo and Fergis walked in. Fergis stopped to sniff a flower arrangement on the counter as Caligo conversed with Madame Ruckus. She pointed to Lumina.

Caligo pulled Fergis toward Lumina's styling chair. "You're the new stylist in town?" he asked.

"Yes, sir. I'm—"

Caligo cut her off. "Whatever. I hear you're a miracle worker. Can you do something with this?" he asked, shoving Fergis toward her.

Lumina nodded. "Absolutely."

"Good luck," Caligo replied meanly. "You'd be the first." Then he stormed out of the salon.

Lumina studied Fergis. He seemed shy, unsure of himself. "I'm Lumina," she said softly. "Would you like to take a seat?"

Fergis remembered his manners. "Oh, of course. Thank you." He sat in the chair as Lumina draped a styling cape around him.

"Is that a Robena Graniflora?" he asked,

staring intently at a potted plant on Lumina's station.

Lumina shrugged. "I'm not sure," she said. "Hey, Cora, what kind of plant is this?" she called to Cora at the nail station.

Cora looked up and cocked her head. "Green?" she ventured. Clearly she didn't know any more about plants than Lumina did.

Fergis looked from the plant to Cora. Lumina noticed he couldn't stop staring at her. "She's beautiful," he whispered.

"I'll introduce you when we're done," Lumina said with a wink.

Fergis settled in comfortably, and Lumina summoned her pearls.

A short while later, Lumina kept her promise. Fergis, with a spiffy updated haircut, followed her across the salon to Cora's nail station.

"Hello, I'm Fergis," he began, nervously extending his hand.

"I'm Cora," she said with a warm smile.

"Do you like plants?" Fergis asked.

"Uh . . . I have a fern," she replied.

"You do?" Fergis cried, overly excited to have something to talk about with her. "Have you ever tried feeding it a mix of bonemeal and phosphorus? It does wonders for the seedlings!"

"I'll give that a try," Cora replied, raising an eyebrow at Lumina.

Lumina stepped away. She hoped a friendship between them might bloom. Fergis sure seemed to need one.

As the town clock chimed five o'clock, Madame Ruckus turned the sign on the salon door to CLOSED. Sandrine, Cora, and Lumina put away their styling equipment for the day. Kuda lent a helping hand.

Once everything was tidy, Madame Ruckus gave the word. "All right, ladies—time to get ready for the ball!"

Excitedly, the girls set to work. They dragged out the plain-Jane dresses they had bought on their lunch break. They started with Sandrine's first, and then Cora's. Lumina showed them how to turn a boring dress into a showstopping gown. She added ribbons, gems, flowers, and seashells to give each gown a personal touch.

Once she had finished, Sandrine and Cora tried their gowns on. They twirled in front of the mirror, marveling at Lumina's exquisite detailing.

Lumina tapped her chin with her pointer finger, thinking. "Maybe one last thing." She rummaged through her styling station and pulled out a couple of jewels. She pinned a small, jeweled rosette on each dress and stepped back. "There! Perfect. You two look fantastic!" she exclaimed.

Madame Ruckus nodded her approval. "Now, put on your sunglasses, ladies, and prepare to be blinded by fabulous!" She swept into the next room to change into her ensemble. Once dressed, she sashayed through the door, covered head to tentacles in jewels and glitter.

Lumina smiled and shielded her eyes. It really was blinding!

The girls clapped their hands with delight.

"Thank you," Madame Ruckus said graciously. "Don't hate me because I'm beautiful."

Everyone cracked up.

"Okay, Lumina, we do your gown next!" Cora said, as the town clock struck eight. Everyone froze.

"Oh no!" Lumina cried. "The ball has started! You guys go and I'll catch up with you there. I insist."

Sandrine, Cora, and Madame Ruckus eyed each other.

Finally, Sandrine spoke. "You never got a dress, did you?" she asked gently.

"Oh, I'm fine—really," Lumina sputtered. She didn't want them to worry about her and miss the ball.

But Kuda, her oldest and dearest friend, knew better. She knew Lumina always put everyone else first. She also knew that deep down Lumina would be heartbroken to miss her chance to attend the ball.

"No, she didn't. She got busy with clients;

she never had time," Kuda answered.

"But does that mean you're not going to the ball?" Cora asked.

Lumina shook her head. "I've been waiting to see the castle all my life. I'm not going to let something like a gown stop me," she replied bravely.

Madame Ruckus rubbed her jaw in thought. Lumina was her best stylist. And she had a heart as big as her own. She couldn't let Lumina flounder. "Ladies," she commanded, pointing her tentacles in eight different directions. "Grab everything you can find here that's made of fabric!"

The girls and Kuda raced to action.

Lumina blushed. "No, really, you don't need to," she protested.

But the fins were already set in motion.

"I'll get the shampoo capes!" Cora called.

"I'll grab the drapes and curtains!" Sandrine shouted.

"The pink and purple are the prettiest," Madame Ruckus noted.

"I'll pick out the trimmings!" announced Kuda, piling seashells, gold ribbons, and jewels onto a nearby table.

"But . . . ," Lumina protested. She didn't want her friends to go out of their way for her. But on the inside, her heart swelled like a song.

CHAPTER 12

Just past eight, the ball was in full swing. Mercouples waltzed to a band playing on a balcony above the dancers. A grand staircase descended on one side of the room, and everything glittered with jewels and scalloped seashells. At the far end of the room, the king and queen's throne sat waiting for them at the center of a long table on a stage.

Cora and Sandrine danced next to a large dessert table covered with cupcakes and pastries of all shapes and sizes. Spike stood near them, sampling the sweets.

"Yoo-hoo!" Fergis shouted from across the room. "Cora!"

Cora waved and watched him approach. As he got nearer, she smelled something funny.

Fergis looked down at the flower corsage on her wrist. "The Robena Graniflora!" he gasped with excitement.

Cora nodded. She had added it at the last moment in honor of her new friend, Fergis.

"It's radiant!" Fergis gushed. "And so are you."

Cora blushed.

"I wore a flower, too," Fergis continued. It's a—"

Just then, Caligo stormed over. He wore a pearl-studded dress uniform. "Fergis!" he bellowed. "Why aren't you dancing?! You're supposed to be finding a bride!"

Fergis hung his head. He had really been enjoying his conversation with Cora. He didn't want to think about all of the rules his father had set for him tonight. "I've tried, Father," he said with a sigh. "Really, I have. But no one will dance with me. They mostly swim away screaming when I get near."

Caligo leaned in toward his son and sniffed. "Whew!" he cried, plugging his nose. "No wonder! What is that stink?"

Fergis puffed out his chest proudly and pointed to his boutonniere. "Oh, that's my Quidest Fetere," he explained, touching the flower on his uniform pocket. "It's quite rare, you know. In fact, you can only find it—"

"Well, lose it," Caligo interrupted in a thunderous voice. He grabbed the boutonniere and crumpled it in his hand. "Now get out there and dance!" he commanded, dumping the crushed flower in a nearby planter.

Fergis hung his head miserably.

Cora was worried. She moved toward him and spoke softly. "Does your father always speak to you that way?"

"What way?" Fergis asked sadly. The music began to play again, snapping him out of his pout. "Oh, there's the music. Excuse me. Father says I have to go dance."

Cora placed her hand gently on his arm. "You know, *I* like to dance," she said.

Fergis looked surprised. "Really? You wouldn't mind?" he asked.

Cora smiled and took his hand. "And I thought your flower was beautiful," she said as they began to waltz.

🐚

Meanwhile, in the ballroom beverage closet, a white-gloved butler unlocked a cabinet. He pointed to a row of bottles, giving instructions. "Their Majesties will be drinking merberry nectar reserve tonight. Be certain you serve them first. Is that understood?"

"Perfectly," Scylla answered, rubbing her hands together.

🐚

Back in the ballroom, the party continued. But someone was missing.

"What happened to Lumina?" Cora asked Sandrine, who was dancing next to her and Fergis.

"As far as I know, she's still outside with Kuda admiring the castle," Sandrine replied.

Suddenly, the crowd gasped and grew silent.

All eyes turned toward the grand staircase.

Cora and Sandrine looked up and saw Lumina floating gracefully down the stairs. Madame Ruckus and Kuda trailed behind her. Lumina wore a pink-and-purple gown studded with shimmering pearls. Around her neck she had fastened a glistening jewel and pearl necklace. She looked magical.

"Girl sure knows how to make an entrance," Sandrine said in awe.

As Lumina glided down the stairs, she tried to take everything in. She had always dreamed of seeing the castle, but she had never imagined she'd actually be attending a royal ball! It was breathtaking.

"Kuda. It's . . ." Lumina felt at a loss for words.

"I know," Kuda replied.

Just then, a man in a pearl-studded uniform swept across the room to greet them. Lumina remembered him from the salon. He was her client Fergis's dad.

"Miss Lumina, welcome! I must thank you. You did absolute wonders with Fergis. I almost didn't recognize him," he said, pausing. "And then, sadly, I did."

Lumina winced. "You're welcome?" she tried.

Just then, a familiar voice stepped in. "I call the first dance."

Caligo bowed and backed away. "Of course, Prince Delphin."

The prince whirled Lumina onto the dance floor.

"Prince Delphin?" Lumina asked, shocked. "And you deliver hair supplies, too?" She thought back to when she had first met Delphin as a delivery boy at Salon La Mer.

"Well," the prince replied, winking. "It's more of a hobby than anything else. When I'm not performing my more princely duties."

"You're joking with me," Lumina replied with a smile.

"And what about you?" Delphin continued. "Hairstylist by day, princess by night?"

"Princess? Who, me?" said Lumina, blushing

at such a silly thought. "I'm the farthest thing from a princess."

Delphin gave a sly smile. "Now who's joking?" he asked with a twinkle in his eye.

Lumina laughed as the prince twirled her around the dance floor. To think that just two days ago she was playing princess with Kuda at the sea cave, and here she was now, dancing with an actual prince! She could hardly believe her good fortune.

Caligo stepped out onto the empty castle terrace. He looked nervously at the town clock tower. Almost time. He turned to enter the castle. "Arrgggh!" he cried, jumping with fright.

Murray swung from the doorway and cackled, pleased to have scared Caligo once again. "Sorry," he hissed. "Everything going as planned?"

"Like clockwork," Caligo replied, recovering himself. "Their Majesties will grace us with their presence fifteen minutes from now—for what will be the king's final appearance. What about the girl?"

"We're zeroing in," Murray said. "Every crawly creature in town is now looking for a seventeen-year-old blond girl named Lumina. Don't worry, we'll get her."

"Named what?" Caligo whispered fiercely, yanking Murray by the collar.

"Lumina," Murray said unsurely. "It was on her note."

Still clutching Murray by the neck, Caligo looked back into the ballroom. "Is that her?" he asked, pointing a finger toward Lumina spinning around the dance floor.

"Um. Why, yes, it would seem so," Murray managed in a choked voice, feeling Caligo's grip tighten. "You found her! And all on your own, too!"

Caligo's eyes narrowed with menace. His plan was coming together.

Inside the ballroom, the music came to a stop. Prince Delphin and Lumina applauded for the musicians.

"Dancing in the castle," Lumina said with a happy sigh. "I never would have believed it."

"Why not?" Delphin asked. "You dance as if you've done it a hundred times."

"Thank you." Lumina giggled.

"I'll get us some refreshments," Delphin offered. "Promise me the next dance."

"I promise," Lumina replied.

The band struck up its next number. Lumina tapped her fingers to the beat as she waited for the prince to return. Then someone grabbed her wrist and yanked her roughly toward the dance floor.

Lumina was shocked. "Uh . . . Mr. Caligo," she began awkwardly, trying to free her hand. "Prince Delphin made me promise to dance with him next. But I can promise you the next—"

Caligo gripped her wrist tighter and twirled her toward the terrace. "Tell me, Miss Lumina," he began with a dangerous look in his eye. "Are you here with your parents?"

Lumina bit her lip. She started to feel nervous. "My parents? Actually, I was raised by my aunt."

"I see. One of life's little secrets," Caligo said with a smirk. "Some secrets, however, are best kept under wraps!" He waltzed Lumina out onto the empty terrace. On Caligo's cue, a mermaid-size sack swooshed down over her from above.

Lumina struggled to break free as the bag scooped her up. She tried not to panic. Then she heard a familiar voice.

"Hey!" Kuda shouted. "What do you guys think you're—"

Whoosh! Lumina heard another sack swoop though the air and then Kuda's muffled cries as she was trapped inside.

"No witnesses!" Caligo cried.

"Where do you want them?" Lumina heard Caligo's partner in crime ask. He sounded slimy.

"The castle dungeon," Caligo replied. "I'll be down in twenty minutes. This time, I'm going to make sure the job is done right."

CHAPTER 13

Moments later, Lumina and Kuda sat miserably on the floor of the dungeon. The bars across the cell looked like teeth in a giant shark's mouth. There was no way to escape. Caligo's eel cronies—Murray, Garth, and Wormwood—guarded them.

"If you ask me," grumbled Kuda, "the only thing eels are good for is sushi."

Garth leaned in and growled at them. *Grrrr.*

Kuda cowered behind Lumina.

"I don't understand," Lumina said to Murray. "What do you want with us?"

"Patience, patience, my dear," Murray hissed. "You'll find out soon enough." He slithered along a stone column.

Something about the way he moved jogged

Lumina's memory. "Wait, I remember you— from the reef. Aren't you a friend of my aunt's?"

Garth and Wormwood giggled.

"Oh, I'd hardly say friend," Murray said. "Your aunt and I are more like business associates."

Kuda raised an eyebrow. Something about this seemed fishy. "Oh, yeah? What kind of business?"

Murray dropped from the ceiling in front of Kuda's face. Kuda jumped.

"We're exterminators of a sort," Murray replied cryptically.

"Yeah!" Garth cried excitedly. "In five minutes, your aunt is going to exterminate the king!"

"Right," Wormwood seconded. "She's going to 'poisonate' him!"

Murray smacked his cronies' heads. Leave it to them to say too much.

Lumina looked concerned. Exterminate? "Aunt Scylla would never poison anyone!" she declared. Would she?

"Lumina, what are we going to do?" Kuda

whispered, staring at the dungeon bars.

Lumina huddled closer to her friend and tried to think. "I don't know," she admitted.

"What do you mean you don't know?" Kuda replied, panicking. "You're always so sure of everything!"

But Lumina wasn't sure about anything anymore. Was her aunt Scylla really going to poison the king? Would Caligo ever set them free? She felt a long way from the safety of the sea cave. Maybe her aunt had been right: the castle was turning out to be a dangerous place. She shook her head. "I'm afraid all is— Wait!" she exclaimed, suddenly coming up with an idea.

"I knew it!" Kuda cried happily.

Lumina unclasped the pearl necklace from around her neck.

"Ah, bribery," Kuda remarked. "Good thinking."

"Not exactly," Lumina replied. She eyed the eels, huddled together, deep in conversation.

Lumina tossed the string of pearls through the cell bars. They landed with a soft thud on the sandy floor. Then she raised her hands and conducted.

Slowly but surely, the string of pearls crept along the floor like a snake.

There's more than one way to out-slither an eel, Lumina thought.

The string of pearls snaked up the opposite wall and, at Lumina's command, wound itself around a ring of keys. *Clank!*

Lumina winced. The eels looked up, but then Kuda coughed, covering the noise.

As the eels returned to their discussion, Lumina made the pearls slink back toward the cell, dragging the keys with them.

Finally, Lumina grabbed the keys through the cell bars. She hid them behind her back.

"Now what?" whispered Kuda. "How do we distract the Noodle Brothers?"

Lumina thought for a minute. Then she plucked a single pearl off her gown. Ready, aim, fire! She flung it at the eels, hitting Wormwood in the back. *Ping!*

Wormwood spun around to face Garth.

"Hey! What did you do that for?" he asked.

"Do what for? I didn't do anything!" Garth replied.

Lumina flung another pearl, this time hitting Murray. *Ping!*

"Ow!" Murray cried, eyeing Garth. "Have you lost your mind?"

Garth held up his hands. "No, I swear! Wormwood must have done it, because I— Ow!" he cried, rubbing his arm where another pearl hit him.

Lumina flung pearl after pearl, pelting the eels. Just like she planned, the eels started fighting one another, pushing, shoving, yelling, and wrestling.

"Cut that out!"

"You started it!"

"Did not!"

"Did too!"

Once they were totally distracted, Lumina seized her chance. She commanded the string of pearls to tie itself into a knot—right around the fighting bunch of eels!

"Hey! What the—?" the eels cried, confused and trapped.

Lumina brushed her hands together and chuckled. "Shall we?" she asked Kuda.

Kuda grinned. "Let's."

Lumina unlocked the cell with the key and they swam out.

"Hey! Grab them!" Murray yelled.

The three eels tried to swim in three different directions, but the pearls knocked them back together.

"You idiots!" Murray screamed, furious.

Lumina conducted the pearls to wrangle the eels into the cell. She slammed the door tight and locked it, then turned toward the exit.

"Come on, Kuda," she called. "We need to hurry!"

The friends raced through the maze of dungeon passageways, trying to find their way back to the palace.

"You don't believe what those slimeball eels said about Scylla, do you?" Kuda asked.

Lumina shrugged. "I don't know what to

believe. But if Aunt Scylla's in some kind of trouble, we've got to help!"

They rounded the corner and spotted two Trident guards.

"Whoa!" Kuda cried, screeching to a halt. She shoved Lumina into an open archway and dove in after her.

The guards floated by without seeing them.

Lumina let out a sigh of relief. The last thing they needed was to be captured and jailed again—especially if Aunt Scylla really was in danger.

"Now what?" Kuda whispered.

Lumina grinned and tossed a few loose pearls into the water. They floated down the hallway toward the guards. One by one, the pearls slipped inside the guards' shirt collars.

Soon, the guards were twitching and giggling as the pearls tickled them. "Now!" Lumina commanded.

She and Kuda raced through the dungeon gate and zoomed through the water, the giggling guards hot on their trail.

CHAPTER 14

As the clock struck nine, Scylla tapped poison silver shavings into a goblet filled with thick syrupy nectar. She set the cup with the others on a heavy silver tray and stepped onto the royal stage. She placed purple goblets in front of where the king and queen would sit, once they were announced. Then she set a black goblet before Caligo, who was already seated.

"Your nectar for the toast, sir," she said flatly.

Caligo gave her a nod as Scylla retreated to the side of the stage. He looked at his goblet and then at the others. Why was his black while all the others were blue? He wondered whether he could trust Scylla. He picked up his goblet and examined it, trying to catch Scylla's eye for some sort of sign.

She didn't give him one. Caligo thought for a moment and then switched his goblet with the king's. He smiled smugly at Scylla. He wouldn't let her get the best of him—not this time. And certainly not when he was paying her handsomely to do the job his way. But still, he felt worried. He switched the goblets back again.

Scylla didn't blink.

Caligo started to sweat.

Satisfied that Caligo was worried, Scylla carried her tray back to the beverage closet. As she refilled a pitcher with nectar, she heard voices from behind a nearby curtain. Curious, she moved a little closer to listen and recognized them as the king's and queen's.

"Nereus, I'm just not sure I can do this," the queen whispered, sounding upset.

"I know, Lorelei, I know," the king said, comforting her.

"We wanted so much for the Pearl of the Sea and the kingdom to someday go to our little girl." The queen sounded like she was choking back tears. "I just wish that she were here.

She would have grown up to be such a bright, beautiful girl." She broke down in sobs.

"It's been hard, very hard," the king agreed. "But we have a duty to our people. Try to be brave."

Just then, a butler walked by. He looked at Scylla's tray and shook his head. "Come, woman! That nectar belongs to the king and queen. You should be serving it right now!"

"Oh," she said, saddened by the conversation she'd just overheard. "Oh, yes, you're right. You're very right. And I've been very wrong— about everything!" She shoved her tray into the butler's hands and made her way to the curtain shielding the king and queen. She had to explain!

A burly guard blocked her way. "Sorry, ma'am. No admittance."

"I must speak to the king and queen," Scylla pleaded. "I have something that belongs to them—and I should have returned it a long time ago."

The guard crossed his arms firmly. "Then you'll have to wait until after the ceremony. The king and queen do not wish to be disturbed."

Scylla blew out her breath in frustration. "Okay, I'll wait. But what can't wait is—"

She zipped toward the stage without finishing her sentence. At the royal table, she reached over Caligo's shoulder for his black goblet. "Give me that, Caligo," she whispered. "I'm done poisoning people."

Caligo snatched his goblet back, holding it tight. "Aha! So I was right! No thanks, I'll just hang on to this one if you don't mind."

Scylla tried to pry it from his grasp. "Caligo, I'm trying to save your—"

"Oh, I know what you're trying to do. You think I'm a fool?" He yanked the goblet, forcing Scylla to let it go.

"Fine," Scylla said, resigned. "It's your funeral."

Caligo smiled. "She thinks she can outsmart me," he mumbled to himself. "Unless that's just what she wants me to think." He looked uncertainly at the goblet in front of him and started to sweat.

Suddenly, trumpets sounded, announcing the

entrance of the king and queen. Caligo, Fergis, and the other special guests at the table rose out of respect. Everyone on the dance floor turned to face the stage as the Seagundia national anthem rang through the air.

The king and queen entered grandly from behind their curtained-off area. The king held his wife's hand regally, and both wore painted-on smiles. Two Trident guards walked in behind them. The crowd bowed, and the royal couple nodded before taking their throne at the table.

"Caligo, is this my cup?" the king asked, pointing to the purple goblet at his place.

Caligo bit his nails in a panic. "I don't know!" he shouted, wiping sweat from his brow.

The king gave him a curious look and rose to address the crowd. "Loyal citizens of Seagundia," he began. "We gather here today to present our kingdom's most treasured symbol, the Pearl of the Sea."

Behind him, a guard brought forth the medallion, nestled on a velvet pillow. The king raised the medallion for the crowd to see. "We present the Pearl of the Sea to a fine young lad who will one day inherit our throne." He turned toward Fergis, who was inspecting a potted plant next to him.

Caligo elbowed his son.

"Oh, right," Fergis said, rising awkwardly. He stepped forward to receive the honor.

The king draped the Pearl of the Sea medallion around Fergis's neck. "And now, a toast!" he declared, holding his purple goblet in the air.

The crowd applauded, and Caligo looked at his own black goblet nervously. He had to pick it up to toast with the king, but what if Scylla had given him the poison instead of the king?

"Come on, Caligo," the king urged, noticing that his brother-in-law was the only one who had not raised his glass. "Will you not toast your own son?"

Caligo stood and, hand shaking, lifted his glass. The king continued, "Citizens, honored guests! To the future ruler of Seagundia, who will someday guide our kingdom's destiny! To my nephew, Fergis!"

"To Fergis!" the audience echoed.

The king and guests lifted their glasses to drink. Caligo panicked. He knocked the king's goblet out of his hand, making it look like an accident. Dark nectar spilled everywhere, oozing like chocolate syrup. Caligo saw Scylla gasp from the crowd.

"Oh, forgive me! I'm so sorry!" he apologized. "Please, Your Majesty—take mine," Caligo finished, offering the king his suspicious black goblet. He eyed Scylla.

"No!" Scylla cried, racing toward the king.

CHAPTER 15

Lumina and Kuda burst into the ballroom just as Scylla lunged for the king's goblet.

"Aunt Scylla!" Lumina cried, horrified.

"The eels were right!" Kuda moaned.

The king raised his goblet to his lips. "Again, let us toast—to Fergis!"

Lumina couldn't let the king drink her aunt's poison. She rushed the stage as the Trident guards chasing her reached for her tail. She knocked the goblet from the king's hand.

The crowd gasped.

Seeing an opportunity, Caligo stood and pointed an accusing finger at Lumina. "She tried to attack the king! Guards, arrest her!" he shouted.

Caligo's guards swooped down and grabbed

Lumina. Suddenly, Madame Ruckus, Prince Delphin, Sandrine, Cora, and Spike rushed the stage to protect their friend.

"Now wait just a minute!"

"That girl never hurt anyone!"

"You can't take her!"

"Unhand her!"

Desperate to explain, Aunt Scylla made her way through the crowd. "Let her go!" she cried. "She saved the king! There was poison in his cup!"

The room went silent. All eyes focused on Scylla.

"Poison? How do you know that?" the king demanded.

Lumina watched as her beloved aunt took a deep breath.

"Because I'm the one who put it there," Scylla admitted, hanging her head with shame.

The crowd buzzed with the news.

Caligo smiled sinisterly. All attention was on Scylla—which meant no one suspected him. He was going to get away with it! Feeling giddy, Caligo stepped back from the crowd. He bumped into Spike, knocking a pearl from one of the stonefish's spikes. Spike didn't even feel it.

Lumina couldn't stand by and watch her only family member be blamed for such a vicious act. "No! Don't listen to her!" she cried, zooming to her aunt's side. Even if Scylla had been involved, Lumina knew she was a good person deep down. There had to be more to the story.

"Old woman," the king thundered, ignoring Lumina's pleas, "why would you want to poison me?"

Scylla shook her head. "I didn't want to. I was forced to. Forced to by—"

As Scylla turned to point at Caligo, he discreetly shoved her—right into Spike. Scylla tumbled backward, landing right on the stonefish's exposed poisonous spike!

Scylla shrieked in pain. Then she collapsed.

"Aunt Scylla!" Lumina cried. She hurried to her aunt's side and knelt down.

"She fell on a stonefish spike!" Sandrine cried.

"Poor woman," Madame Ruckus said, clucking her tongue. "That venom will finish her."

Caligo moved through the crowd. "You heard the old woman," he shouted. "She tried to poison our beloved king! And if this girl knew"—he pointed a finger at Lumina—"she must be an accomplice. Take her away!"

Lumina looked up pleadingly at Caligo. "Please, sir. Just give us a moment."

The guards stepped forward, but Kuda blocked their path. "Back off!" she hollered.

Sandrine, Cora, Madame Ruckus, Spike, and Delphin filed in behind Kuda, ready to defend Lumina.

"The lady said give her a moment," Madame Ruckus ordered through clenched teeth.

Lumina cradled her aunt in her arms. "Aunt Scylla, please stay with me. Please be all right."

Aunt Scylla struggled to whisper. "Lumina, I need to tell you—"

"No," Lumina interrupted. "Save your strength."

But Scylla was determined that Lumina know the truth. It was time. "Long ago," she began weakly, "I took you from your parents. I did it to protect you. But all these years they were suffering. I should have told them, but I was afraid of losing you. Please forgive me." Scylla's body fell limp.

Lumina choked back her tears. She turned to Spike. "Spike, your venom—there must be an antidote! Something that can cure her?"

Spike wiped a tear from his own eye. "I'm sorry. There's only one thing I know of—the Sulfer Lily. But it's extremely rare. I've never even seen it."

Lumina hung her head. What would she do without her aunt? Then she heard a gasp from the crowd and Cora's voice.

"Fergis?" she asked, seeing Caligo's son jumping up and down excitedly. "Do you know that plant?"

"I—" Fergis started. Then he locked eyes with his father and cowered. "N-no," he stammered.

Caligo smiled darkly. "Then the old woman's done for. Nothing we can do."

Out of the corner of her eye, Lumina saw Cora whisper to Fergis. Fergis looked from his father to Cora and back again.

Caligo saw it, too. "You heard the boy!" he thundered. "He said it's hopeless."

Then Fergis stepped forward. "No, Father, it isn't. The Sulfer Lily is the common name for Quidest Fetere. And there's one right here." He reached into a nearby potted plant and retrieved his crumpled up boutonniere! He waded through the crowd toward Lumina.

"Thank you, Fergis," Lumina said.

"Just two petals on Scylla's tongue," Spike instructed.

In the background, Lumina heard Caligo yell, "You fool, Fergis! You could have been king!"

"I keep telling you, Father," Fergis replied firmly, "I don't want to be king. I want to be a botanist!"

Lumina caught Cora beaming with pride at Fergis.

"Guards! Grab them!" Caligo thundered again.

Trident guards appeared at every corner and closed in on Lumina, Scylla, and Fergis.

Chapter 16

"Don't you touch her!" Lumina ordered as the guards surrounded her. She would not let them take the only family she had. Determined, she closed her eyes and focused her energy. She summoned every single pearl in the ballroom to her command.

Pearls flew toward her from hairdos, clothes, and thrones. They flew off Spike's spikes and down from chandeliers. The pearls swarmed toward Lumina, swirling into a tornado of protection around her and Aunt Scylla. They glowed brightly, pulsing with shielding energy.

The crowd looked on, amazed and stunned into silence. Even Caligo was speechless for once. He watched the pearls adorning his own uniform pop off and fly to Lumina's command.

The pearls formed a blanket for Scylla to lie on. Then they lifted her into the air.

The guards backed away, terrified. Lumina noticed the king and queen looking adoringly at her. Why did they suddenly seem familiar? She shook her head and focused again on the task at hand. As Scylla hovered in the air, Fergis gently placed the petals on her tongue. "Stay with me, Aunt Scylla. Please stay with me," Lumina whispered.

Bathed in a glow of swirling pearls, Aunt Scylla gradually opened her eyes—a tiny bit at first, and then wider. She smiled.

Lumina's heart swelled. "Aunt Scylla!" she cried with happiness.

Lumina's friends cheered all around her.

The pearl whirlwind died down. The pearls scattered and floated away as their owners tried to reclaim them. Spike replaced his pearls with the help of Madame Ruckus's eight arms.

Lumina helped Aunt Scylla to her feet. She was still very weak.

The king moved toward her. "Miss," he began

tentatively. "Tell me, the way you made those pearls move—how?"

Just then, Caligo stepped in and cut him off. "Your Majesty, what we've just seen proves how dangerous these two are! As commanding general, I insist on placing them both under arrest."

The king raised his hands in protest. "Wait a minute, Caligo. I want to ask the girl—"

"It was him!" Scylla interrupted. She pointed at Caligo. "He was the one who ordered me to poison Your Majesty! He wanted the throne for his son!"

"The old mermaid is delusional!" Caligo shouted. "Arrest these women—and all of their traitorous friends!"

The Trident guards moved toward Lumina and her friends. But Madame Ruckus was ready. She squirted them with a cloud of black ink!

"Hey! I can't see!" cried one of the guards.

"Where did they go?" shouted another.

"Lumina, get out of here!" Madame Ruckus ordered. "Kuda, you too!"

But Lumina couldn't leave all of her dear friends behind to fight her battle. "Not a chance!" she cried as Kuda head-butted a guard. Lumina whipped off the pink pearl belt she had fastened around her ball gown. She hurled it toward the captain of the guards. It wrapped around his tailfin and cinched, yanking him upside down!

Spike rolled himself into a ball and bowled over two more guards. Sandrine whacked a group of guards with her massive tail, sending them flying. Delphin decked a guard with his fist. Madame Ruckus spun in a circle, using all eight of her arms to slap guards away like a pinwheel gone haywire. The frightened crowd in the ballroom backed off.

Lumina watched as Caligo raced toward the exit. She raised her hands and sent hundreds of pearls to block his path.

"Out of my way!" Caligo growled, spinning to find another way out.

Lumina cut him off. "How about that dance I promised?" she challenged. She summoned more pearls to surround Caligo and lift him straight into the air. She sent him sailing backward.

"*Ahh!*" Caligo shrieked as he slammed into a wall. He slid down to the floor, dazed.

Madame Ruckus jumped on top of him, holding him down with all eight tentacles.

The king signaled for the palace guards. "Imprison these traitors!" he ordered.

The guards seized Caligo and the Trident Squad and marched them off.

Chapter 17

Lumina wiped her brow. It felt good to see Caligo finally locked up where he couldn't harm anyone else. She breathed a sigh of relief. Then she heard a soft voice by her side. She turned to see the queen looking questioningly at her.

"The pearls . . . Have you always been able to do that?" the queen asked.

Lumina shrugged. "Sure, I guess. Why?"

The king joined his wife and took her hand. "Because you have the royal gift—the pearl magic," he explained. "Is it possible? Could you be our daughter?"

Lumina knitted her brow. She was confused. The pearl magic was always something she just had. She never thought she'd find a reason for it. Was the king suggesting that she was royalty? She felt light-headed.

"She is your daughter," Aunt Scylla said.

"I—I am?" Lumina didn't understand.

The king and queen threw their arms around Lumina, wrapping her into a group hug.

Lumina locked eyes with Scylla, silently asking her if it all was true. Scylla nodded.

Lumina beamed, feeling warm inside as so many of her questions were finally answered.

"But how?" the king asked, pulling back to examine Lumina at arm's length.

"Caligo again," Scylla explained. "Years ago, he paid me to do away with your daughter. But I couldn't do it. So I raised her instead—away from him."

Lumina took it all in. Suddenly, everything made sense: Scylla had wanted her to stay near the sea cave to keep her safe from Caligo!

Just then, Fergis approached. "In that case," he began, holding out the Pearl of the Sea medallion, "I think this is Lumina's."

The king took the medallion and placed it

around Lumina's neck. As he did, the pink pearls on Lumina's dress turned white and began to glow brightly. The queen placed a sparkling pink tiara on Lumina's head.

The crowd cheered. Their princess had returned!

"Your Majesties," Scylla continued, "I am so, so sorry for keeping her from you all these years. I thought I did it to protect her, but the truth was I just couldn't give her up."

Lumina felt a lump form in her throat. Aunt Scylla had loved her and cherished her as if they were true family. And in Lumina's heart, that meant that they were—and always would be.

"The important thing is that she's here now," the king replied. "Lumina, welcome home."

Lumina looked around the grand ballroom. She thought about the castle that stretched before them in every direction. "Home?" she asked. "You mean the castle? Here?" It was a dream come true! She wrapped her arms around the king and queen, who hugged her right back.

Lumina was still struggling to take it all in.

"So you're my father?" she asked the king.

"Yes," he replied.

"And you're my mother?" she asked the queen.

"Yes."

"And this is home?" Lumina said.

"Yes!" the king and queen both replied, laughing.

Lumina beamed. Then she remembered something. "But," she began, frowning at the thought, "it won't be home if Aunt Scylla and Kuda aren't here with me."

Kuda jumped up and down excitedly. Scylla looked worried.

"No," Scylla protested. "It wouldn't be right."

The queen took Scylla by the arm. "Of course it would," she insisted. "You saved her. You're her family, too."

Scylla's eyes glistened with tears. "You'll see," she said to the queen, looking at Lumina. "She leaves things a little better than she found them—starting with my heart."

The women embraced, and Lumina joined

them in another group hug.

The king chuckled. "But this is still a royal ball, is it not? And now it's a homecoming as well. Music, maestro, please!"

The royal band struck up a waltz, and the king and queen began to dance.

Lumina watched her parents twirl gracefully around the floor. Then a finger tapped her on the shoulder. She turned to see Prince Delphin.

He held out his hand. "In that case, I believe you owe me a dance . . . Princess."

Lumina grinned. "As promised," she replied.

They joined Cora and Fergis, Sandrine, Madame Ruckus, Spike, and Kuda out on the dance floor.

Lumina looked around at all the friends she had made and the family—both new and old—who loved her. Each one of them, in their own special way, shone brighter than any pearl. And that, Lumina knew, was the best dream come true of all.